In Our Neighborhood

Meet a Firefighter!

by AnnMarie Anderson
Illustrations by Lisa Hunt

Children's Press®
An imprint of Scholastic Inc.

SCHOLASTIC

Special thanks to our content consultants:

Anthony Scali
Firefighter
Ladder Company 123
Crown Heights, NY

James Slevin
Firefighter
New York City, NY

Library of Congress Cataloging-in-Publication Data
Names: Anderson, AnnMarie, author. | Hunt, Lisa, 1973– illustrator.
Title: Meet a firefighter!/AnnMarie Anderson.
Other titles: Meet a firefighter!
Description: New York: Children's Press, an imprint of Scholastic Inc., 2021. | Series: In our neighborhood | Includes index. | Audience: Ages 5–7. | Audience: Grades K–1. | Summary: "Two children learn the important role of firefighters in their neighborhood"—Provided by publisher.
Identifiers: LCCN 2020031731 | ISBN 9780531136867 (library binding) | ISBN 9780531136928 (paperback)
Subjects: LCSH: Fire fighters—Juvenile literature.
Classification: LCC HD8039.F5 A43 2021 | DDC 363.37092—dc23
LC record available at https://lccn.loc.gov/2020031731

Produced by Spooky Cheetah Press
Prototype design by Maria Bergós/Book & Look
Page design by Kathleen Petelinsek/The Design Lab

Printed in North Mankato, MN, USA 113

1 2 3 4 5 6 7 8 9 10 R 30 29 28 27 26 25 24 23 22 21

Scholastic Inc., 557 Broadway, New York, NY 10012.

Table of Contents

OUR NEIGHBORHOOD

Hi! I'm Theo. This is my best friend, Emma. Welcome to our neighborhood!

Over there is the fire station. Today we are going to the fire department's annual chili cook-off. We can't wait to meet some firefighters!

MEET FIREFIGHTER SARAH

When Emma and I got to the fire station, we met a firefighter named Sarah. She took my chili over to the contest area. Then she offered to show us around.

The United States has more than one million career and volunteer firefighters. Almost 100,000 of them are women.

Sarah took us inside the fire station and introduced us to firefighter José. He explained that some firefighters work 24-hour shifts. They stay at the fire station while they wait for calls to come in. The firefighters have their meals together. There's even a place for each person to rest.

The housewatch room is near the front door. The firefighter on duty sees who goes in and out of the station and waits for calls.

Then Sarah took us into the engine bay. "If a call comes in when we're upstairs in the bunk room, we slide down that pole," she said. "It's the fastest way to get to the engine bay. That's where we get dressed."

Sarah showed us how her pants are turned out over her boots to save time. She steps into her boots and pulls up her pants and suspenders in one move.

Next Sarah took us outside to see the trucks. Other firefighters from the company showed us some of their vehicles.

When firefighters arrive at a fire, they connect a hose to the fire hydrant. They use a special five-sided wrench to open the hydrant. The water flows to the pump, then goes to the firefighters' hoses.
On a quint truck, this pump panel controls the flow of water through the hoses.

Firefighter Sarah told us firefighters use a lot of different cool vehicles to fight fires.

Fireboats are used to fight fires on the water and also on land near the water.

Fire motorcycles can get to the scene of an emergency faster than a large truck can. They are used during crowded events such as parades and fireworks shows.

Wow! I didn't know you used anything other than fire trucks.

Helicopters drop water and chemicals that slow the spread of forest fires.

It takes a lot of special equipment to do our jobs.

Small airplanes carry firefighters called smoke jumpers into hard-to-reach areas.

As we were walking back to the picnic area, we saw some firefighters practicing a drill.

"We do training exercises all the time," Sarah explained. "Practice helps us know exactly what to do in an emergency."

Firefighters practice lifting and carrying life-size dummies.

FIRE SAFETY

We got some chili and sat down. "Firefighters aren't the only ones who need practice," Sarah told us. "You should have fire drills at home and school, too." I told her that my family has a home escape plan. Now we know what to do in case of a fire.

"That's great," she replied. "And remember: Stay close to the floor and crawl if there is smoke. Make sure doors aren't hot before you open them. And always close doors behind you."

If your clothing catches fire, cover your face with your hands. Then stop, drop, and roll to put the fire out.

Your home should have a working smoke alarm and carbon monoxide detector in every bedroom and on every floor.
“We had a fire once while my mom was cooking dinner,” Emma told us.
I was scared, but I stayed calm.

"My mom told me to get my brother, go outside, and call 911. Then she used a fire extinguisher to put out the fire."

SEARCH AND RESCUE

As Emma finished her story, we heard a shout. A woman had cut her hand with a knife. A firefighter rushed over with a first aid kit.

First aid isn't just for people! Pets sometimes need medical care after a fire or another emergency.

"Firefighters do more than fight fires," Sarah told us. "We have first aid training so we can help people who are hurt."

"Wow!" said Emma. "Firefighters have a lot of skills."

"That's true," Sarah replied. "We are called to act in all sorts of emergencies."

"If someone is trapped in a car after an accident, we can help."

"We are trained to rescue people who have fallen through ice."

"Firefighters also rescue people and animals trapped in floodwaters after a hurricane."

Then firefighter José came outside to announce the cook-off winner. "Theo is our winner," he said. "His chili set our taste buds on fire!"

My prize was the chance to sit in the cab of a fire truck. I got to turn on the siren and the horn. It was the perfect end to an amazing day!

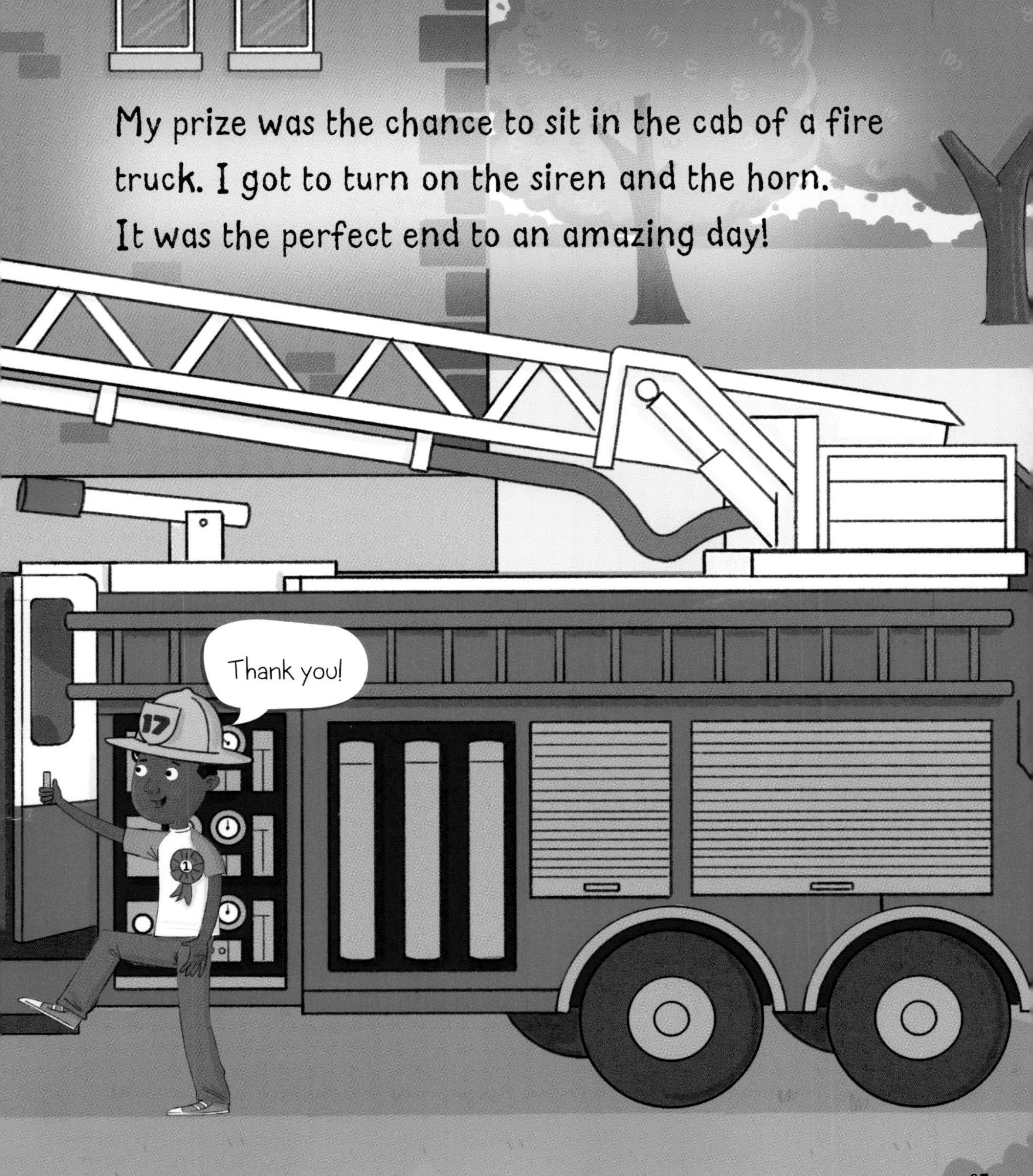

Ask a Firefighter

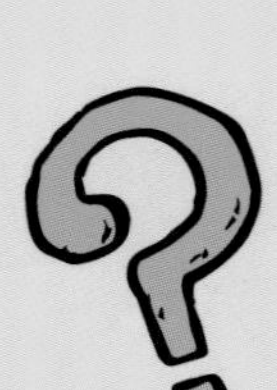

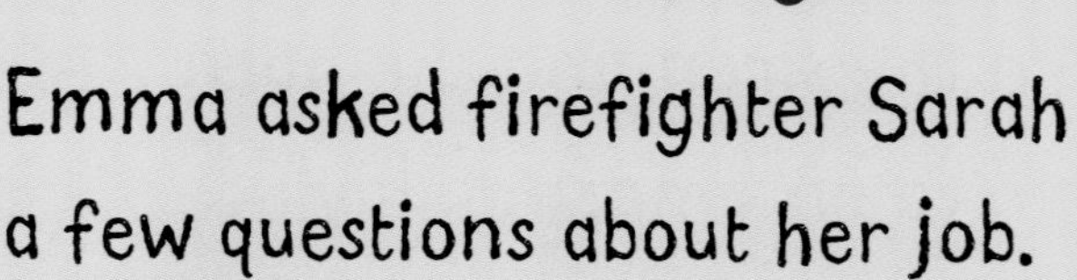

Emma asked firefighter Sarah a few questions about her job.

What did you do to become a firefighter?

After completing high school, I had to pass a challenging written exam and a physical exam. Then I trained for nearly 500 hours before I began working at the fire station.

Do you get any sleep when you are on duty?

It depends on the night. In between calls, I might lie down and close my eyes for a few hours.

What is the hardest part of your job?

Training never stops! Firefighters are always learning new things. We have to stay healthy and remain in good shape at all times.

What is the best thing about your job?

The friendship of the other firefighters. We support and take care of one another.

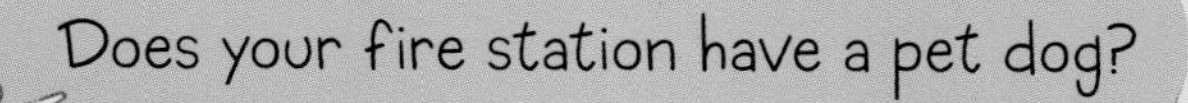

Does your fire station have a pet dog?

We don't, but some fire stations do keep dogs as pets.

Firefighter Sarah's Safety Tips

- Never play with matches, candles, lighters, or fire.
- Test smoke alarms and carbon monoxide detectors each month, and change batteries twice a year. Check the fire extinguisher monthly. Its needle should point to the green "charged" zone.
- Make an escape plan at home and school. Practice getting out! Have a meeting place away from your house, apartment building, or classroom.
- If there's a fire, get low and go. Don't try to take your favorite things with you. Never go back into a burning building.
- Don't hide from firefighters! Their equipment might look scary, but they are there to help.

A Firefighter's Tools

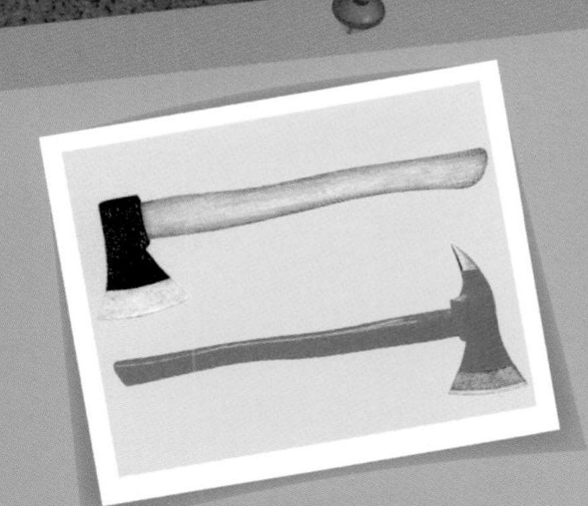

Ax: Firefighters use an ax to break through doors.

Bunker gear: This gear includes a firefighter's fire- and heat-resistant boots, pants, coat, and gloves, plus a hard helmet for protecting the head.

Breathing apparatus: This equipment, with its face mask and oxygen tank, provides breathable air for firefighters.

Halligan tool: Firefighters use this three-part tool to pry open doors, break glass, and make holes in walls.

Index

About the Author

AnnMarie Anderson has written numerous books for young readers—from easy readers to novels. She lives in Brooklyn, New York, with her husband and two sons. She loves to (safely) build a campfire for s'mores in the summer!